# Ten in a Bed

# by Jan Ormerod

DK Publishing, Inc.

There were **ten** in the bed,
till Amelia said,

yawn

yawn

yawn

"Time to get up!"

So out she came with
a stretch and a yawn.

yawn          yawn
              yawn

And then there were nine.

9

There were **nine** in the bed,
till Amelia said,

"Big Ted,
you're smelly!"

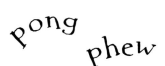

So out he came,
and the diaper went on.

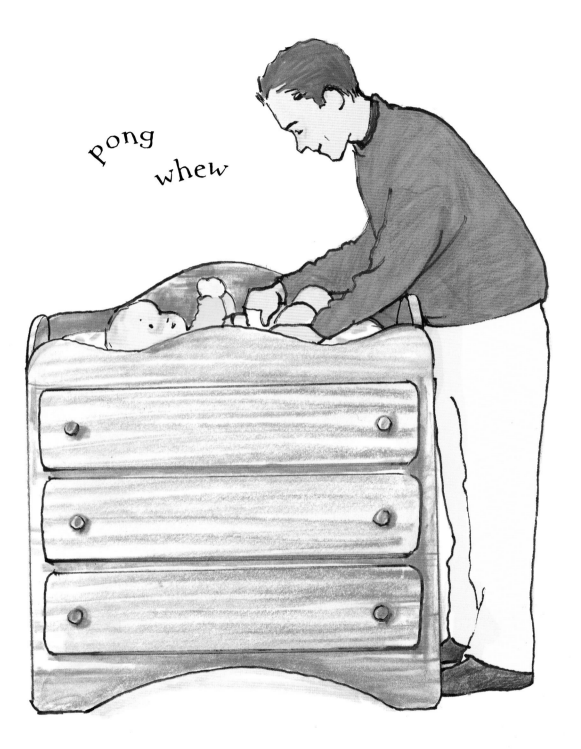

pong

whew

And then there were eight.

8

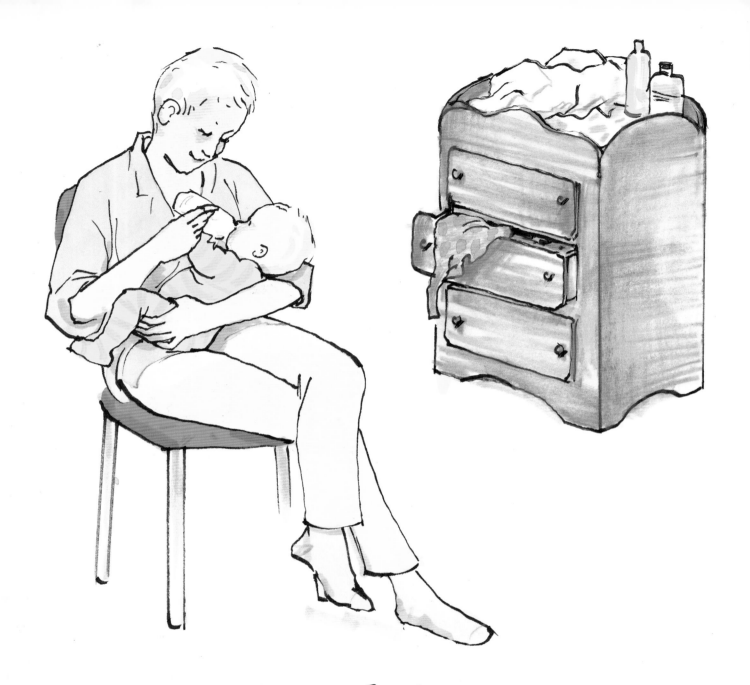

There were **eight** in the bed,
till Amelia said,

"Blue Bird, you're thirsty."
So out she came and
glugged down
her juice.

glug
glug
glug

And then there were seven.

7

There were **seven** in the bed,
till Amelia said,
"Come on, Baby, it's bathtime!"

So out she came for
a splash in the tub.

Splish!
Splash!
Splosh!

And then there were six.

6

There were
**six**
in the bed,
till Amelia said,

"Rag Dolly, it's time
to get dressed."

So out she came, and
the dress went on.

And then there were five.

5

There were

**five**

in the bed,

till Amelia said,

"Panda, mashed carrot surprise!"

So out he came with a spit
and a splatter.

Slurp, slurp

And then there were four.

4

There were **four** in the bed,

Wheeeeeeeeeee!

till Amelia said,

"Pink Pig, it's playtime!"

So out she came, and they whizzed through the air.

And then there were three.

3

There were **three** in the bed,
till Amelia said,

"Monkey,
let's go for
a walk!"

So out he came,
and they all set off.

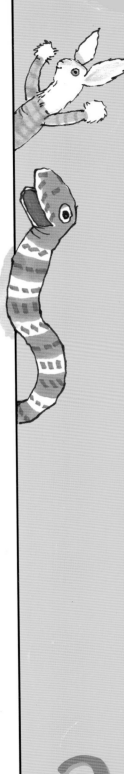

And then there were two.

2

There were
**two**
in the bed,
till Amelia said,

"Snake, it's
storytime!"

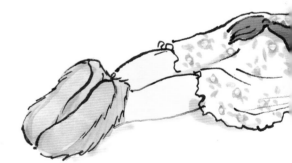

So out he came for
a book and a hug.

Again!
Again!

And then there was one.

1

There was **one** in the bed,
till Amelia said,

"Mr. Bunny, I'll sing you a song."

La la la la la la

So out she came for a sweet lullaby.

And then there were none.

There were **lots** in the bed
and Mommy and
Daddy said,

"There are too many in this bed!"

But none came out,
and they all
snuggled up.

Night-night!
Sleep tight!

# Other Toddler Books to collect:

Good-bye, Hello!
Silly Goose and Dizzy Duck Hunt for a Rainbow
Baby Loves Hugs and Kisses
Baby Loves
My Do It!
Ball!
Ned's Rainbow
Hide and Sleep
One Smiling Sister
Ting-a-ling!
Grumble-Rumble!
Here Comes the Rain
Grandma Rabbitty's Visit
Silly Goose and Dizzy Duck Play Hide-and-Seek

LONDON, NEW YORK, SYDNEY, DELHI, PARIS,
MUNICH, and JOHANNESBURG

First American edition 2001
Published in the United States by DK Publishing
95 Madison Avenue, New York, New York 10016

01 02 03 04 05 10 9 8 7 6 5 4 3 2 1
Text and illustrations copyright © 2001 Jan Ormerod

Library of Congress Cataloging-in-Publication Data
Ormerod, Jan.
Ten in a bed / written and illustrated by Jan Omerod. – 1st American ed.
p. cm. – (Toddler story books)
Summary: As her parent take care of the baby, Amelia acts out each activity, from feeding to bathing, with one of her ten toys until only one is left on the bed,
and then it's time for Amelia's bedtime story.
ISBN 0-7894-7863-3 – ISBN 0-7894-7864-1 (pbk.)
1. Babies – Fiction. 2. Parent and child – Fiction. 3. Toys – Fiction. 4. Counting 1. Title. II. DK toddler story book.
PZ7. O634 Te 2001     E  – dc21    2001028504
Color reproduction by Dot Gradations, UK. Printed in China by South China Press

see our complete
catalog at
**www.dk.com**